A DINOSAUR ATE MY HOMEWORK

RAY NELSON JR,
DOUGLAS KELLY,
& BEN ADAMS

with the cooperation of Raymond T. Rye,
National Museum of Natural History, Smithsonian Institution

BEYOND
WORDS
Publishing
I N C

For Alexandria and Ben...the littlest Rhinos

ABOUT FLYING RHINOCEROS BOOKS

Flying Rhinoceros books are dedicated to the education and entertainment of elementary school students. **Flying Rhinoceros also offers curriculum/activity packs to accompany all of the books.** For more information or to request a catalog, please contact Beyond Words Publishing, Inc.

Beyond Words Publishing, Inc.
4443 NE Airport Road
Hillsboro, Oregon 97124-6074
503-693-8700
1-800-284-9673

Designed by Christy Hale
Printed in Hong Kong
Distributed to the book trade by Publishers Group West
ISBN: 1-885223-35-8 14.95 hardcover

Library of Congress Cataloging-in-Publication Data

Nelson, Ray, 1965-
      A dinosaur ate my homework / by Ray Nelson, Jr.,
Douglas Kelly & Ben Adams.
           p. cm.
      Summary: Facts about different kinds of
dinosaurs accompany a story about a boy who brings
various prehistoric animals to school for show-and-tell.
      ISBN: 1-885223-35-8
      [1. Dinosaurs–Fiction. 2. Schools–Fiction. 3. Stories in rhyme.]
I. Kelly, Douglas, 1955- . II. Adams, Ben. III. Title.
[PZ8.3.N3644Di   1996]
96-8535
[Fic]–dc20
CIP
    AC

OTHER BOOKS FROM FLYING RHINOCEROS:

The Seven Seas of Billy's Bathtub (Ocean and sea life)
Connie & Bonnie's Birthday Blastoff (Outer space)
Wooden Teeth & Jelly Beans: The Tupperman Files (U.S. presidents)
Greetings From America: Postcards from Donovan & Daisy (U.S. geography)
The Flying Rhinoceros Cartooning Kit (How to draw cartoons)

ACKNOWLEDGMENTS

Flying Rhinoceros Productions, Inc., would like to thank Raymond T. Rye for his assistance in preparing this book. Mr. Rye has been the information officer for paleontology at the National Museum of Natural History, Smithsonian Institution, for 19 years. In addition, he teaches both physical and historical geology at George Washington University.

Flying Rhinoceros Productions, Inc., would also like to thank the following for their participation in making this project come to life: Julie Mohr, Kari Rasmussen, Stephanie Taylor, Mike and Holly McLane, Chris Nelson, Theresa Nelson, Ji Yun Kim, Jeff and Katherine Nuss, Jacie Pete, Edna Nelson, Paul and Joan Craig, Deborah Beilman, Ray Nelson, Sr., and the SunWest crew.

This is a tale of a rather odd chap,
who not long ago caused quite a flap.
Earl P. Sidebottom is the name of this boy
who thinks being strange is rather a joy.

He likes to wear bow ties; it suits his weird taste.
He snorts when he giggles and likes to eat paste.
Everyone knows he is smarter than smart.
He has an IQ that jumps off the chart.

Homework, you know, makes most kids feel queasy,
but for our hero Earl, it's really quite easy.
Then one fateful day when homework was due,
Earl looked worried, he really looked blue.

He told Mrs. Snodgrass with a sniff and a snort,
"A giant T. rex ate my report!"
Mrs. Snodgrass looked Earl right in the eye
and huffed, "Little boys never should lie."

"It isn't a fib, cross my heart, hope to die,"
Earl continued, "I really did try!
I had just finished writing about the
    Boston Tea Party,
        when I heard a gruff voice say,
            'Hey, Mr. Smarty...'

                As quick as I could...
                I turned my big head,

                to spy a
                DINOSAUR
                    on top of my bed!"

3

He said, 'Little boy, I want something to eat,
and that paper you're holding looks like a treat!'

I ran for the door with a zippity zoom,
but now there were dinos all over my room.
I was in a tight spot, I couldn't retreat...
So I tossed them my homework and let them all eat."

Mrs. Snodgrass chuckled and gave a mocking reply,
"I think I can help if you just let me try.
For our class Show-and-Tell, bring your dinos to school,
and I'll sit them all down and tell them the rule.
You dinos may be hungry and ready to eat,
but Earl's finished homework...

IS NOT FOR A TREAT!"

The very next day
Earl gave a great cheer.
He could soon do his homework
without any fear.

Snodgrass will help,
with nary a fuss.
The hard part will be...
getting seats on the bus!

WHAT IS A DINOSAUR?

Dinosaur means "fearfully great reptile."
Dinosaurs were a group of animals that lived millions of years ago.
They laid eggs and were covered with scales. Dinosaurs came in
all shapes and sizes. Some of them were gigantic, bigger than a
house. Others were as small as a chicken. Some dinosaurs were
peaceful plant-eaters while others were flesh-eating hunters.

Nobody has ever seen a live dinosaur but we know that
dinosaurs existed because scientists have discovered and
pieced together fossils.

WHAT IS A FOSSIL?

A fossil is evidence of life from the earth's past. For example, when a
dinosaur or prehistoric plant died, the remains were often covered
by layer after layer of dirt, sand, and mud. Gradually the surrounding
minerals filtered into the remains and turned them into rock. After
thousands of years, the once living thing has become a fossil of stone.

"Now settle down, class,
and please take your seats.
It's Show-and-Tell time
and you're in for a treat.
I've got plenty to tell,
but first let me show
some dear friends of mine
from a long time ago."

TIME PERIODS

PALEOZOIC ERA

CAMBRIAN PERIOD

(600 million years ago) Life started in the sea.

CARBONIFEROUS PERIOD

(363 to 290 million years ago) For more than 70 million years, trees and plants filled the earth's swampy lowlands. Fossils of the earliest reptiles have been found in holes left by stumps that decayed after floods killed the trees.

PERMIAN PERIOD

(290 to 257 million years ago) Reptiles began to develop.

MESOZOIC ERA ("Age of the Reptiles")

TRIASSIC PERIOD (257 to 208 million years ago)

The climate was mild and warm. Prehistoric reptiles lived in the air, in the sea, and on land. At the end of this period, many reptiles became extinct but new ones took their place. The most successful were the dinosaurs.

MNOPQRSTUVW XYZ

JURASSIC PERIOD

(208 to 146 million years ago)

Newly-formed seas brought rain to the coastlines and plants began to grow in areas that had been deserts. These new forests and jungles provided large amounts of food for the dinosaurs. Dinosaurs ruled the land.

CRETACEOUS PERIOD

(146 to 65 million years ago)

The land masses began to look like the continents that we know today. Flowering plants appeared for the first time. There were many different kinds of dinosaurs and small mammals. The end of the dinosaurs came with the end of the Cretaceous Period.

CENOZOIC ERA

TERTIARY PERIOD

(65 to 1.5 million years ago)

Mammals spread and diversified. Grazing mammals and flightless birds appeared. In this period many different kinds of mammals roamed the earth.

QUATERNARY PERIOD

(1.5 million years ago to today)

Large mammals and modern humans arrived on the scene.

TODAY

As Earl continued with his Show-and-Tell bash,
mountains were growing from lava and ash.
Swamps began forming in the front parking lot,
and the weather turned muggy, humid, and hot.

13

JUST WINGING IT...

Pteranodon was a
"flying reptile." Its body
was the size of a turkey but
its wings measured over 20
feet long from wingtip to wingtip.
The largest flying animal ever
was *Quetzalcoatlus*. While
each of its wings was as
long as a bus, the entire
reptile weighed only
about 100 pounds.

Pteranodon

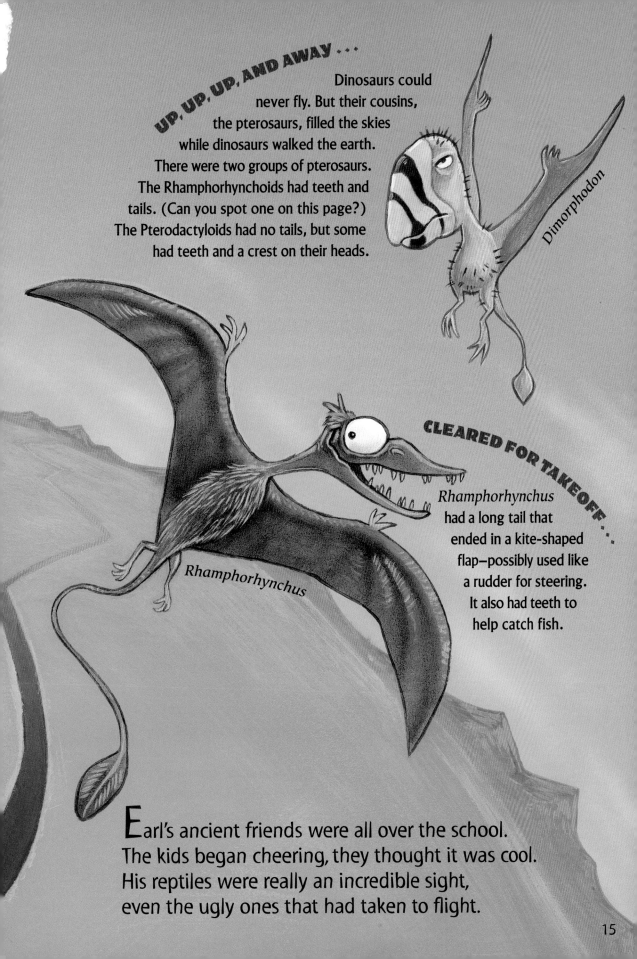

Dinosaurs could
never fly. But their cousins,
the pterosaurs, filled the skies
while dinosaurs walked the earth.
There were two groups of pterosaurs.
The Rhamphorhynchoids had teeth and
tails. (Can you spot one on this page?)
The Pterodactyloids had no tails, but some
had teeth and a crest on their heads.

Dimorphodon

CLEARED FOR TAKEOFF . . .

Rhamphorhynchus
had a long tail that
ended in a kite-shaped
flap—possibly used like
a rudder for steering.
It also had teeth to
help catch fish.

Rhamphorhynchus

Earl's ancient friends were all over the school.
The kids began cheering, they thought it was cool.
His reptiles were really an incredible sight,
even the ugly ones that had taken to flight.

15

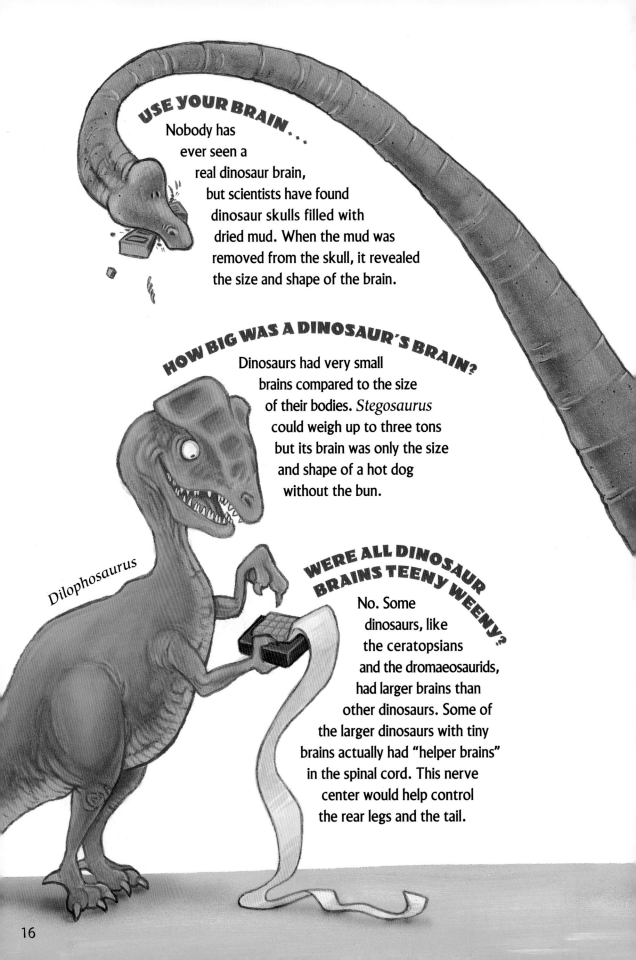

USE YOUR BRAIN...

Nobody has ever seen a real dinosaur brain, but scientists have found dinosaur skulls filled with dried mud. When the mud was removed from the skull, it revealed the size and shape of the brain.

HOW BIG WAS A DINOSAUR'S BRAIN?

Dinosaurs had very small brains compared to the size of their bodies. *Stegosaurus* could weigh up to three tons but its brain was only the size and shape of a hot dog without the bun.

Dilophosaurus

WERE ALL DINOSAUR BRAINS TEENY WEENY?

No. Some dinosaurs, like the ceratopsians and the dromaeosaurids, had larger brains than other dinosaurs. Some of the larger dinosaurs with tiny brains actually had "helper brains" in the spinal cord. This nerve center would help control the rear legs and the tail.

Some dinosaurs rambled to room 106,
where students watched on as they did dino tricks.
They answered math questions as right as the rain,
except for the big guy with the peanut-sized brain.

TWO OR FOUR?

Flesh-eaters, like the *Dilophosaurus*, walked on two legs so they could use their hands to hold onto their prey. Some smaller plant-eaters walked only on their hind legs, too. The giant plant-eaters, like *Diplodocus*, needed four legs underneath them to support their massive body weight.

BIPED— ("two-footed") An animal that walks on its two hind feet.

TWO AND FOUR...

Some dinosaurs spent time on either four or two legs. The *Corythosaurus* walked, rested, and escaped from predators on two feet. It stood on all four legs when it ate low-growing plants.

Diplodocus

17

HOT, HOT, HOT!

"Warm-blooded" creatures (like mammals and birds) have body temperatures of around 100 degrees F. This temperature is maintained by chemically burning food. A warm-blooded creature needs to eat often to stay warm.

BBRRRRRRRR!

A "cold-blooded" creature has a body temperature that changes with its surroundings. If the outside temperature is warm, the creature warms up and becomes more active. As the temperature cools, the animal becomes sluggish. Cold-blooded creatures do not need as much food as warm-blooded creatures to survive.

WARM OR COLD?

We may never know if dinosaurs were warm-blooded or cold-blooded. There are arguments that support both "warm-blooded" and "cold-blooded" theories. Is it possible that dinosaurs were somewhere in between?

FASTER THAN A SPEEDING COMPSOGNATHUS . . .

Many people think of dinosaurs as big, slow, clumsy creatures. Many dinosaurs were, in fact, very fast and agile. The Ornithomimids, for example, were built much like an ostrich. They had long, thin, strong legs and a long neck with a tiny head. The distance between their fossilized footprints tells scientists that Ornithomimids might have reached speeds between 25 and 30 miles per hour.

Compsognathus

Recess was something that sounded like fun—
the dinos could stretch and have a good run.
They played wall ball and tag, and swung on the swing.
They also played dodge ball, which made their heads ring.

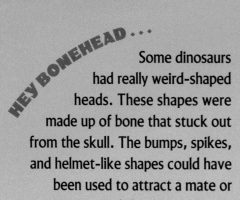

Some dinosaurs had really weird-shaped heads. These shapes were made up of bone that stuck out from the skull. The bumps, spikes, and helmet-like shapes could have been used to attract a mate or to defend against predators.

The long hollow crest on top of *Parasaurolophus'* head was probably used like a microphone, helping the dinosaur to communicate.

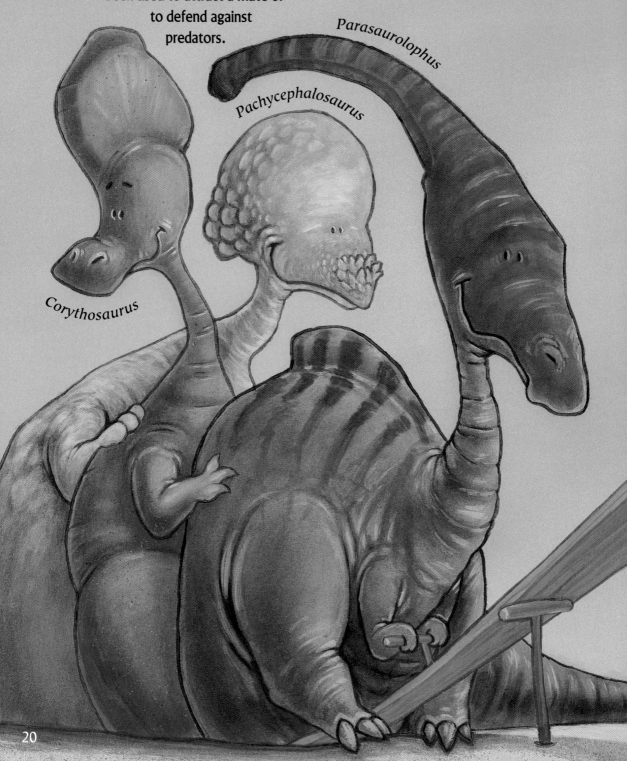

Parasaurolophus

Pachycephalosaurus

Corythosaurus

HEAD BUTT . . .

Pachycephalosaurus
is part of the group of dinosaurs
known as the "boneheads." The skulls
of these dinosaurs were up to 10 inches thick.

Everyone learned on that rather strange day
that dinos are fun...when you get them to play.
The teeter-totter, however, is not very fun
when the guy that you play with weighs over a ton.

The biggest creature ever
to live on land was *Brachiosaurus*.
This plant-eater weighed over
50 tons and was 70 feet long
and 39 feet high. (That's as
big as a four-story building.)
Recently bones were
discovered of a dinosaur
that may actually
be bigger than
Brachiosaurus.
Scientists call this
new dinosaur
Ultrasauros.

BIG, BIG, BIG . . .

Recess was over...
class was soon to begin,
but people were squished
like sardines in a tin.
These dinosaurs came in
and took over the hall—the fat ones,
the skinny ones, the big and the small.
The kids didn't mind,
though the going was slow.
But it was really annoying
if they stepped on your toe.

Saltopus

SMALL,
SMALL,
SMALL...

Some
dinosaurs
were
quite
small...
Saltopus
was only
about two
feet long,
weighing
two pounds.
(That's about
the size of a
chicken.)

Many of the dinosaurs really liked art,
so they picked out some paper and got ready to start.
But the paper kept tearing. What was the cause?
You can't finger-paint with razor-sharp claws.

BIG BAD CLAW *Deinonychus* was one of the most vicious
dinosaurs to walk the earth. It stood five feet
tall, weighed about 150 pounds, and probably hunted in packs.
This dinosaur was incredibly fast and smart and had
a giant claw on each foot. When the
Deinonychus attacked, the razor-sharp
claws would slash and
slice the unlucky
prey.

Deinonychus

CLAWS...

Flesh-eating predators had narrow, curved, sharp claws, which were used to grab onto and kill prey. Plant-eating dinosaurs had broad, flat claws that may have been used to dig for food.

FOOTPRINTS...

When dinosaurs walked in soft ground they left deep footprints. The footprints dried and filled with sand, dirt, and mud, eventually becoming "trace fossils." A trace fossil is not actually part of a dinosaur, but is evidence of one.

Stegosaurus

Brachiosaurus

Apatosaurus

WHAT'S ON THE MENU?

WHERE'S THE SALAD BAR?

Many dinosaurs were plant-eaters and had special "tools" to help them eat all kinds of tough plants. Some had beaks that snapped off parts of plants; others had powerful jaws and hundreds of sharp teeth to grind up the plants. The Sauropods would swallow plants whole. The plants may have been ground up by big "gizzard stones" in the stomach.

GIZZARD STONES?

Gizzard stones are small, round pebbles swallowed on purpose to help grind up food in the stomach.

FLYING RHINO CLUB

26

MAY I HAVE SECONDS ON WIENER WRAPS?

There was a group of dinosaurs that chased, killed, and ate other dinosaurs. All of these flesh-eating dinosaurs are part of a group called Theropods. The carnosaurs were Theropods that had big heads, strong back legs, and short arms. They walked on two legs and were not very fast, but had powerful jaws full of razor-sharp teeth. *Tyrannosaurus rex* was a carnosaur.

Another group of flesh-eaters was the coelurosaurs. They were small and fast and had long, narrow jaws.

Tyrannosaurus rex

The dinosaurs really looked forward to lunch, although they chose different lunches to munch. Some of the creatures picked veggies to eat, while all of the others chose to munch meat.

Braincase

Cervical vertebra

Scapula

Humerus

HIP, HIP, HOORAY!

Scientists have divided
dinosaurs into two groups by studying
their skeletons. The first group is the
Saurischia, or "lizard-hipped" dinosaurs, which
included both flesh-eaters and plant-eaters. They had
hip bones that pointed downward, as seen in lizards of today.

The second group is the Ornithischia,
or "bird-hipped" dinosaurs, which were
all plant-eaters. They had hip bones that pointed
down and backward, as seen
in birds of today.

Lizard   *Bird*

Metatarsus

The students all learned about dinosaur bones,
as the classroom filled with low reptile moans.
A rather small guy spoke up at the scene,
"These bones make me nervous, if you know what I mean."

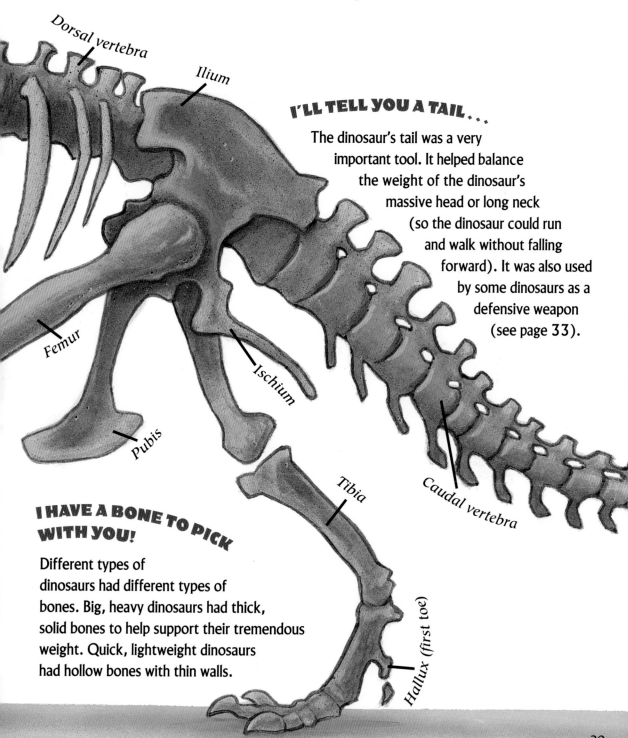

Dorsal vertebra

Ilium

I'LL TELL YOU A TAIL...

The dinosaur's tail was a very
important tool. It helped balance
the weight of the dinosaur's
massive head or long neck
(so the dinosaur could run
and walk without falling
forward). It was also used
by some dinosaurs as a
defensive weapon
(see page 33).

Femur

Ischium

Pubis

Tibia

Caudal vertebra

I HAVE A BONE TO PICK WITH YOU!

Different types of
dinosaurs had different types of
bones. Big, heavy dinosaurs had thick,
solid bones to help support their tremendous
weight. Quick, lightweight dinosaurs
had hollow bones with thin walls.

Hallux (first toe)

WHICH CAME FIRST . . . THE DINOSAUR OR THE EGG?

Dinosaurs laid eggs just like birds and reptiles do today. Fossilized eggs have been found in large dinosaur nests. Some were found with unbroken eggshells and unborn dinosaurs inside! Skeletons of hatched baby dinosaurs have also been found, still in the nest.

MOTHER, MAY I . . .

Maiasaura ("good mother reptile") fossils were discovered in 1978 in Montana. The discovery answered questions about how dinosaurs raised their young. Skeletons were dug up along with fossils of eggs, nests, and actual baby dinosaurs. Several nests were found together, which suggests these dinosaurs nested in a colony.

EGGS . . .

Each nest that was dug up in Montana had 15 to 20 eggs in it. The eggs were partially covered by sand, which could mean that the parents covered the eggs to keep them warm.

OMELETTES ANYONE? If a dinosaur egg were proportionate to a dinosaur's size, it would be too thick for the babies to breathe or break out of. A sauropod's egg could be up to 10 inches long, or about twice the size of an ostrich egg. The eggs found in Montana are about eight inches long.

Just down the hall, a crowd gathered 'round.
The science room filled with a loud cracking sound.
There appeared a small head and two tiny legs
from a dinosaur nest and some dinosaur eggs.

CLEAN YOUR PLATE!

Stegosaurus had two rows of bony plates that stood up on its back. Since these plates could not have provided much protection, it is uncertain what purposes they served. Most experts think that *Stegosaurus* was cold-blooded (see page 18), so the plates might have helped give the creature more surface area so that the sun could warm its blood faster.

TOOT YOUR HORN!

The Ceratopsians, or horned dinosaurs, were among the last dinosaurs to walk the earth. These dinosaurs had a large, bony frill extending around their necks. Attached to their neck frill were powerful muscles that operated their enormous lower jaw. The most famous of this group was the *Triceratops* ("three-horned face").

Stego

Students in music enjoyed a real treat.
Some reptiles jammed with a dinosaur beat.
They tooted their horns and pounded their tails,
drummed on their plates and practiced their scales.

DUHHH! *Stegosaurus* had one of the smallest brains of any dinosaur. It was about the size and shape of a hot dog without the bun. That is pretty amazing since *Stegosaurus* was 20 feet long and weighed up to three tons.

SCARY TALE!
Some dinosaurs used their tails for protection. *Stegosaurus* had spikes on the end of its tail, while the *Ankylosaurus* tail was like a large bony club. The Sauropods used their massive tails like whips.

Triceratops

All of the kids loved a good swim,
but the pool was too full and they couldn't jump in.
One little girl thought it would be hard
if a dino had trouble while she was lifeguard.

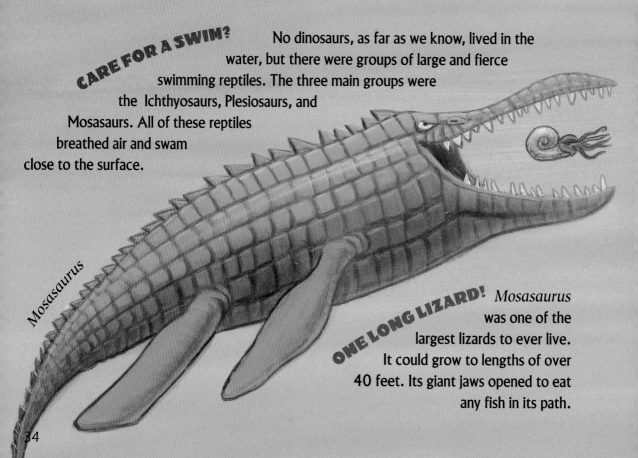

CARE FOR A SWIM? No dinosaurs, as far as we know, lived in the water, but there were groups of large and fierce swimming reptiles. The three main groups were the Ichthyosaurs, Plesiosaurs, and Mosasaurs. All of these reptiles breathed air and swam close to the surface.

Mosasaurus

ONE LONG LIZARD! *Mosasaurus* was one of the largest lizards to ever live. It could grow to lengths of over 40 feet. Its giant jaws opened to eat any fish in its path.

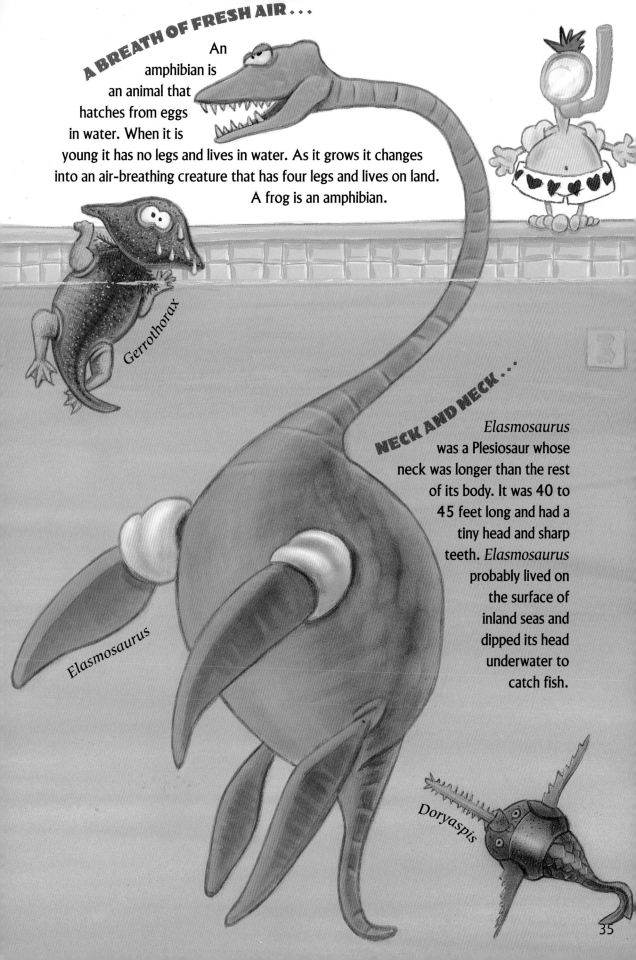

A BREATH OF FRESH AIR . . .

An amphibian is an animal that hatches from eggs in water. When it is young it has no legs and lives in water. As it grows it changes into an air-breathing creature that has four legs and lives on land. A frog is an amphibian.

Gerrothorax

Elasmosaurus

NECK AND NECK . . .

Elasmosaurus was a Plesiosaur whose neck was longer than the rest of its body. It was 40 to 45 feet long and had a tiny head and sharp teeth. *Elasmosaurus* probably lived on the surface of inland seas and dipped its head underwater to catch fish.

Doryaspis

35

Earl went to the bus
at the end of the day.
Time to head home...
time to go play.
He stood on the step
and looked all around,
but his dinosaur friends
were not to be found.

Maybe now Earl's problems
would finally cease.
He could finish his homework in
absolute peace!

It seems the dinos were in a wee bit of trouble—
the school had been turned into a big pile of rubble.
The flagpole was bent, and the pool had a leak.
The doors were all dirty and their hinges were weak.

Footprints were left up and down the main hall,
and it seemed like the walls would soon take a fall.
The unruly herds acted crazy and wild.
These dinos were worse than any small child.

The vice-principal saw them. She hollered and yelled,
"Get over here, before you're expelled!
Go to my office! Do it now! Move your feet!
Don't mess around! Hurry up! Take a seat!"

"Detention, my friends,
is where you'll spend your time,
not near volcanos or swamps full of slime.
So get ready to take a rather long walk.
Follow me now, and bring lots of chalk."

39

You can search through the night
and search through the day,
but you won't find a dino
who will come out and play.

Most people think it's because they're all dead,
but I'd like to offer this reason instead.
Dinosaurs aren't hiding beneath
the mud and the sands—
they're in a small classroom,
with chalk in their hands.
They must pay the price
for all of their crimes,
writing "I will behave"
...10 billion times!

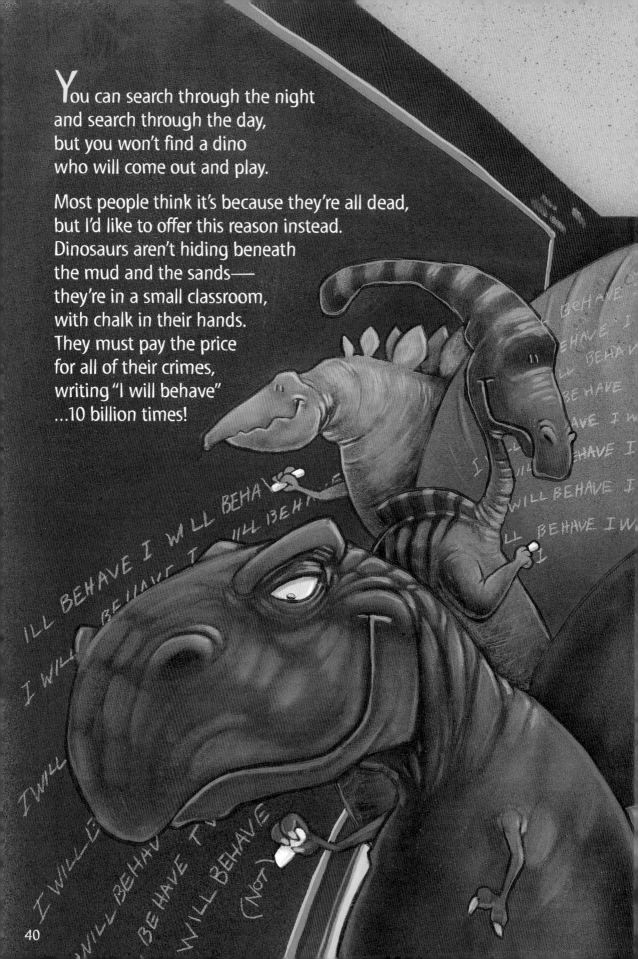

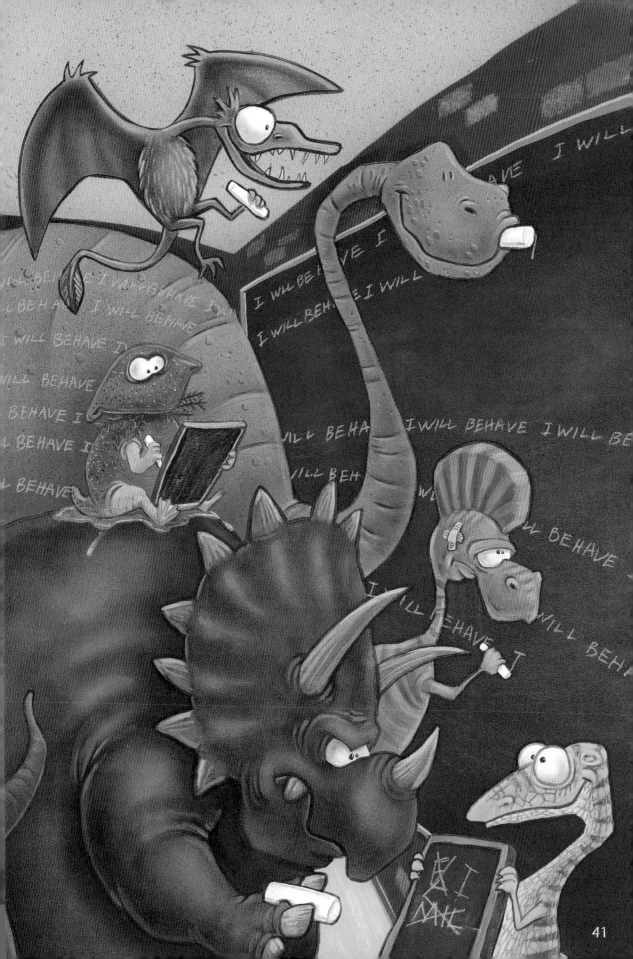

MRS. SNODGRASS' CLASS

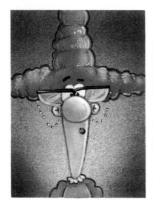

Mrs. Snodgrass

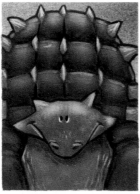

Ankylosaurus
ann-Kye-low-SOAR-uss
"Fused Reptile"

Apatosaurus
uh-PAT-oh-SOAR-uss
"Deceptive Reptile"

Brachiosaurus
Brack-ee-oh-SOAR-uss
"Arm Reptile"

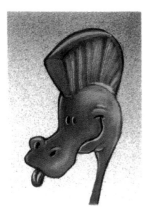

Corythosaurus
koe-Rith-o-SOAR-uss
"Helmet Reptile"

Dilophosaurus
die-Loaf-oh-SOAR-uss
"Two-Ridged Reptile"

Marcus Snarkis

Bonnie Harmony

Connie Harmony

Harvey
Horseburger

Fred Mertz, Jr.

Oviraptor
Oh-vee-RAP-tor
"Egg Seizer"

Joe Kim

Parasaurolophus
Pair-ah-soar-AWL-oh-fuss
"Like a Crested Reptile"

Pteranodon
tair-ANN-oh-donn
"Winged and Toothless"

Penelope Ratsworth

Earl P.
Sidebottom, Jr.

Ruby Snarkis

Spinosaurus
Spy-no-SOAR-uss
"Spiny Reptile"

Stegosaurus
Stegg-oh-SOAR-uss
"Roofed Reptile"

Triceratops
try-SAIR-uh-tops
"Three-Horned Face"

Tommy Tupperman

Tyrannosaurus
tye-Rann-oh-SOAR-uss
"Tyrant Reptile"

Velociraptor
veh-Loss-ih-RAP-tor
"Speedy Predator"

DINOSAUR FAMILY TREE

HERRERASAURIDAE

THEROPODA

CERATOSAURIA

SAURISCHIA

TETANURAE

SAUROPODA

SAUROPODODOMORPHA

PROSAUROPODA

DINOSAURIA

SCELIDOSAURIDAE

THYREOPHORA

STEGOSAURIA

ANKYLOSAURIA

ORNITHISCHIA

PACHYCEPHALOSAURIA

CERATOPSIA

CERAPODA

ORNITHOPODA

DINOSAUR GLOSSARY

Ankylosaur – An armored dinosaur. Bones in the skin of these animals are connected together into great pieces of armor plating.

Armored Dinosaur – There were three groups of armored dinosaurs, which were protected by bony spikes, horns, and plates (pages 32 and 33).

Carnosaurs – A group of large to huge flesh-eating dinosaurs that lived in the Late Jurassic through the Cretaceous period.

Ceratosaurs – A group of flesh-eating dinosaurs with a kinked upper jaw, a crested snout, and separate vertebrae. They had up to four fingers per hand, and a tail that was stiff in the rear half. They ranged in size from small to large, and are found from the Late Triassic through the Cretaceous period.

Ceratopsian – ("horned face") Plant-eating dinosaurs with horns on their face and a bony frill that extended backward from the rear of the skull.

Coelurosaur – A group of small flesh-eating dinosaurs that lived in the Late Jurassic through the Cretaceous period.

"Cold-Blooded" – An outdated term once used to describe an animal with an internal body temperature that is relatively lower than in living mammals, and that changes in response to the temperature of the animal's environment.

Dromaeosaur – Fairly small, flesh-eating dinosaurs with a sickle-like, swiveling claw on the second toe, and a long, stiff tail. This group, which lived in the Late Cretaceous period, includes *Deinonychus*.

Extinction – The death of a species so that it no longer exists anywhere.

Fossil – Any evidence of life from the geologic past. For example, buried bones may be soaked by groundwater carrying dissolved minerals that fill up the spaces where the blood vessels lay and cells of marrow used to live. Such fossil bone is therefore partly composed of real bone and partly of other minerals that have replaced some of the original organic tissue.

Hadrosaur – The group of plant-eating dinosaurs that are also known as duckbills.

Ornithischian – ("bird-hipped") One of the two major groups of dinosaurs, characterized by a pelvis in which the pubis (front bone) was rotated back to lie parallel with the ischium (rear bone).

Paleontologist – A scientist who studies ancient life, exclusive of humans.

Reptiles – Vertebrate animals with skins made of scales, and no free-living larval stage. They hatch in a miniature adult stage from eggs laid on dry land.

Saurischian – ("reptile-hipped") One of the two great groups of dinosaurs, characterized by a pelvis in which the pubis (front bone) was directed forward and down.

Sauropod – ("reptile-foot") A subgroup of the saurischian dinosaurs, the members of which were gigantic plant-eaters with long necks and long tails.

Theropod – ("beast-foot") Flesh-eating saurischian dinosaurs that walked only on their hind feet.

"Warm-blooded" – An outdated term once used to describe living birds and mammals, which maintain a nearly uniform body temperature, generally higher than that of their surroundings.

ABOUT THE AUTHORS

RAY NELSON JR. loves to draw weird stuff and write silly stories. He has been writing and drawing educational books for kids since 1990. Most people find it hard to believe Ray is an author and illustrator. He stands 63 feet tall and weighs 30 tons. (He might be a member of the Sauropod family.) Most people think Ray looks better suited to be a recreational vehicle. Ray currently lives in Portland, Oregon, with his wife, Theresa, daughter, Alexandria, and Molly the mutant dog.

DOUGLAS KELLY

is a very talented painter, snappy dresser, and swell dancer. He is constantly amazing his coworkers with his uncanny ability to break into a medley of show tunes. Most people find it hard to believe Doug is an author and illustrator. He stands two feet two inches tall and weighs 15 pounds. (He is about the size of a *Saltopus*.) Most people think Doug looks better suited to be a speed bump. Doug currently lives in Portland, Oregon, with his friends Victoria and Toonces the cat.

BEN ADAMS joined Flying Rhinoceros Productions, Inc., in July 1994. Ben is really strange, so he has had no trouble fitting in with the rest of the Rhino herd. He has worked for Will Vinton Studios, Walt Disney Studio, and Avia Footwear. He enjoys looking at comic books, scaring small forest creatures, and listening to heavy-metal music. Ben spends his spare time sculpting and doing weird art work stuff.

Jay Dee Alley